When 10-year-old Ben Tennyson stumbles upon a mysterious alien device in the woods one summer, little does he realise that his life is set to change – forever.

As soon as the watch-like Omnitrix quite literally gets a grip on him, Ben discovers it gives him the ability to transform into 10 different alien super-beings, each one with awesome powers!

Using the Omnitrix to cause super-powered mischief turns out to be fun, but will Ben learn to use his might to fight for good?

READ ON AND FIND OUT . . .

MEET THE CHARACTERS

BEN TENNYSON

TEN TIMES MORE TROUBLE
THAN THE AVERAGE KID!

GWEN TENNYSON

RED-HEADED VOICE OF REASON
TO HER COUSIN BEN

GRANDPA MAX

JUST A MILD-MANNERED
GRANDFATHER - OR IS HE?...

VILGAX

ALIEN WARLORD WITH A REAL
ATTITUDE PROBLEM

FOUR ARMS

PROOF THAT FOUR ARMS
ARE BETTER THAN TWO

HEATBLAST

THIS ALIEN'S ON FIRE!

XLR8
HE'S ALWAYS UP TO SPEED

UPGRADE
NEVER HAS A PROBLEM WITH MODERN TECHNOLOGY...

DIAMONDHEAD
YOU COULD SAY HE'S A SHARP SHOOTER

STINKFLY
THERE'S NO FLY SWAT BIG ENOUGH FOR THIS INSECT

GREY MATTER
HE'S A CLEVER LITTLE THING

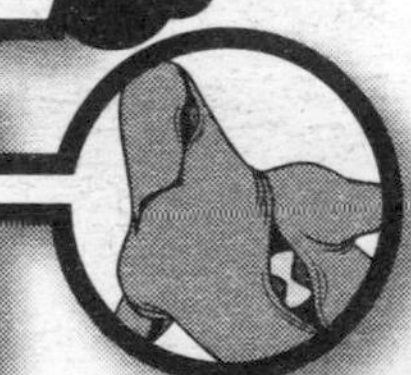

GHOSTFREAK
YOU WON'T FIND HIM BEATING HIS HEAD AGAINST BRICK WALLS

RIPJAW
NEVER BITES OFF MORE THAN HE CAN CHEW

WILDMUTT
HE'S ONE DOGGIE YOU SHOULDN'T PET!

EGMONT
We bring stories to life

Published in Great Britain 2008
by Egmont UK Limited
239 Kensington High Street, London W8 6SA

Adapted from the animated series by
Glenn Dakin

ISBN 978 1 4052 4468 8

5 7 9 10 8 6

A CIP catalogue record for this title is available from
the British Library

Printed and bound in Great Britain by the CPI Group

BEN 10™
THE ALLIANCE
+
SECRETS

BEN 10™
THE ALLIANCE

CHAPTER ONE
HANDS UP!

Sleek and menacing, an enormous spaceship moved into orbit round the planet Earth. Its armoured hull bulged with weapons beyond human imagination. A hatch opened and two probes were fired out into space. Inside the

control room, a bug-eyed robot turned to face its master.

'The drones have launched,' said the robot second-in-command, 'equipped with improved tracking systems. They should be able to find the Omnitrix.' A yellow light glowed from a huge metal pod in the centre of the control room, and a creepy voice emerged from within.

'They may find it, but retrieving it will not be easy,' rasped the voice. It sounded half alien, half robot, and all evil. 'Whoever has the Omnitrix continues to be an opponent of extreme danger and inspiring brilliance.'

In a petrol station shop down on Earth, the owner of the Omnitrix was about to show just how brilliant he was. Ben Tennyson, after a long, hungry road trip, had the munchies. He reached out for a box of cookies – from bang in the middle of the display pile.

CRASH! The mountain of cookie boxes fell right down on Ben's cousin Gwen.

'Smooth move, Tennyson,' she groaned, her green eyes flashing. Gwen was used to disasters – both major and minor – whenever her cousin Ben was around. And she knew how to treat them – with typical sarcasm.

The two looked like any other pair of ordinary kids. Gwen was a smart redhead with a cool attitude, in blue sweatshirt and jeans. Ben was a bright-eyed ten-year-old, with a mop of shiny brown hair, and a white T-shirt with a black stripe down the front.

But one thing made these kids different: the chunky black watch on Ben's right wrist was super-cool alien technology, the Omnitrix. It made Ben a hero – and it also made him, and his travelling companions, a target for trouble.

The two cousins stepped out of the shop, back into the hot dry air of New Mexico. The petrol station seemed deserted, apart from one armoured security van parked nearby.

Up ahead, Grandpa Max was washing the dusty windows of The Rust Bucket – the big six-wheeled motorhome they were using for their trip. He was a grey-haired old guy with a fondness for wearing bright tropical shirts. But this grandpa was a lot tougher than he looked – and a lot cooler too.

He smiled as he spotted the little picture Ben had drawn in the dirt on the window – a grumpy face, along with the words: WASH ME.

'Oh, nice artwork, Ben,' he said.

'You know. Makes a statement,' Ben grinned.

BOOM! In a sudden shuddering blast, the back doors of the armoured van parked nearby blew off their hinges. Flames lit the sky and smoke billowed through the air.

'No,' Gwen said, '*that's* a statement!'

Then they appeared – the gang that

had set up this robbery. Ben checked out the threat. There were three crazy-looking bad guys in biker gear, covered in pointy studs. These wackos had painted monster faces on their helmets and sharks' teeth on their energy blasters. Two of the gang jumped into the back of the armoured car, while the other one stood guard.

'What are you looking at?' The gang's leader, a tough cookie called Joey, suddenly noticed that their robbery had a wide-eyed audience.

'Gwen! Ben! Get back!' Grandpa shouted, pushing the kids behind The Rust Bucket for cover. Joey's gun unleashed a blast of pure energy. Grandpa Max dodged out of the way, but was thrown to the floor by the force of the explosion.

'I've *got* to get Grandpa out of there!' Ben exclaimed. He hit the dial of his watch, blinked in the dazzling green glow and braced himself for the change.

The thieves were emptying the van of bank notes when a giant figure loomed above them in the smoke. They were confronted by an alien – a colossal red-skinned monster – who looked as if he worked out a *lot*. Four Arms stared back at them with four bright-orange eyes.

WHOOM! With one mighty blow, Four Arms smashed the petrol station forecourt, creating a shock wave that threw all three bad guys into the air and landed them in a heap.

'Go!' Four Arms bellowed at Grandpa Max. He hustled to safety with Gwen behind The Rust Bucket. From out of the security van staggered a weedy guard in a blue uniform.

'You OK?' asked Four Arms. The guard took one look at his rescuer and fled, screaming.

'Hmm,' mused Four Arms. 'Wonder if that's a "yes"?'

Then the gang struck back. Joey blasted a petrol pump, igniting the gas tank below. A ball of fire exploded across the forecourt, catching Four Arms off guard.

'Ben!' cried Grandpa Max.

The three thieves looked into the soaring flames, but saw no sign of their attacker. Suddenly, from out of the column of smoke, leaped Four Arms. Landing with the force of a comet he sent Joey, the gang leader, sprawling across the concrete.

Next, Four Arms picked up the other two thieves and hurled them into the side of the armoured car. While they were still reeling, his big red hands plucked off their helmets.

'Huh?' he stopped in surprise. Two startled girls with blue hair and dark lipstick stared back at him.

'You're all women!' Four Arms continued. 'Look, I don't want to hurt you.' Joey appeared behind Four Arms and zapped him right between the shoulder blades.

'Well, isn't that sweet,' she smirked. Four Arms turned to face her. Joey had taken off her helmet, and was revealed as a purple-haired tomboy, with multiple ear-piercings and sulky fat lips.

'Clobber her!' screamed Gwen from behind The Rust Bucket. At that moment, two robot drones flew out of the smoke overhead. Twin lasers ploughed up the garage forecourt and blew apart what was left of the armoured car.

KA-BLAM! Dollar bills came down in a

great paper shower. Joey grabbed two handfuls and scrunched them up in despair.

'Hey, this is *my* heist!' she complained.

'You can have it!' snapped back the other gang members, watching the deadly drones swoop down to renew their attack. They were buzzing around Four Arms like angry mosquitoes.

Joey was too angry at Four Arms to care about the crazy robot attack. While the big red hero was distracted, she levelled her blaster at his back. Grandpa Max grabbed a tyre from a pile nearby and hurled it like a frisbee at Joey's head. **WHUMP!** – it knocked her to the floor.

'Ben, those drones must be after the watch!' Grandpa called out. Joey sprang back up and aimed her blaster at him.

'You'll get yours, old man!' she snarled. The weapon flared to life. Grandpa Max ducked the main blast, but it hit the roof support behind him. Broken concrete tumbled down, sending him crashing to the ground.

'Noooo!' Four Arms roared. This looked serious. The drones attacked again, but they had chosen a bad moment. Playtime was over. Four Arms snatched the flying pests out of the sky and smashed them both together.

'Fly swat!' he growled, hurling the mangled remains at Joey and knocking her off her feet. Four Arms raced to help Grandpa Max up, as Gwen pulled out her mobile phone.

'We need to get him to a hospital,' she

said. 'I'm calling nine one –' Four Arms didn't let her finish. He picked Gwen up in one arm and Grandpa Max in another.

'No time,' he growled. 'Hospital up the street!' With an incredible leap, he bounded away.

Left behind in the smoking rubble, Joey climbed to her feet. She picked up a smashed robot drone and peered at it curiously.

'Who were you freaks?' she wondered. Suddenly, the drone sparked to life. It stretched out a probing arm and stuck it into Joey's throat.

'Aargh!' Joey screamed in pain. She was helpless to prevent what happened next. The drone combined with her body, sending out cyber-organic parts into her system. Powerful robot muscles and sharp metal fins sprang up on her arms and legs. Weapon systems connected themselves to a chip in her brain. Red sense globes grew over her face. She was now half robot and half Joey. In fact, she was now Rojo!

Two police cars pulled up, sirens wailing. Four cops leaped out, guns at the ready.

'Freeze!' one of the men shouted. Rojo no longer had to fear the police – her new computer systems told her that. The drone technology summoned two laser blasters. They morphed into position above Rojo's shoulders, and swivelled to target the cop cars.

'I already did my time,' Rojo said. 'It's time you guys paid!' She blasted the two patrol cars into the air. The astonished cops scrambled out of the line of fire.

'This is going to be a blast!' Rojo smirked.

The city hospital lay on a sunny corner, nestled among rocky desert hills. Inside, Grandpa Max was in good hands. His bandaged head lay on a comfy pillow, and his plastered leg was winched up to help it mend. Gwen and Ben were not used to seeing him like this. They didn't even know that grandpas could break.

'Your grandfather has suffered a severe blow,' the doctor said. 'He'll be out for several more hours. He also has a broken leg.'

Ben looked glum. In the past, they'd always escaped in the nick of time, by amazing heroics or just dumb luck. But this time Grandpa's luck had run out.

'He's going to be OK, right?' Ben asked. The doctor, a kindly man with a neat black moustache and bright blue shirt was quick to calm Ben's fears.

'For a man his age, he's remarkably strong. He'll be fine after some rest.' The doctor glanced down at the patient's notes. 'Now, it says here he was hit by a car bumper. Did someone back into him?'

Ben thought for a moment.

'Actually, the bumper flew through the air after this robot drone blew up the car.' The doctor looked doubtful.

'A vivid imagination can be a good way to cope with a situation like this,' he said, patting Ben on the shoulder as he walked away. Ben looked back at his grandfather, lying unconscious in bed. For once, he couldn't laugh this adventure off. He had some thinking to do.

Up in space, Vilgax was receiving the latest report from his robotic second-in-command. As usual, where the Omnitrix was concerned, the news wasn't good.

'The drones were destroyed,' the robot said. Vilgax seethed inside his recovery pod – the special chamber that repaired and maintained his alien body.

'Send out more!' he barked.

'We may not need to,' the robot replied. 'It seems the drones have somehow merged. I'm receiving one combined signal. And that signal is on the move.'

'Hmmm,' Vilgax paused to consider this surprising report. This was interesting. 'Perhaps one head is better than two.'

In the centre of town, screaming shoppers fled from the jewellery store. Rojo was out to pick up some bling, and she wasn't planning on using her credit card. She surveyed the store, her red sense-globes glowing. Her laser beam cut a perfect circle through a glass display case full of diamond rings. Rojo gleefully grabbed the booty – then cried out as she heard a horrible **SCRUNCH**. Her metal claws had crushed the precious jewels to dust!

'Noooo! They're worthless now!' she cried. She turned in rage, and stomped towards a terrified shop assistant. Suddenly, Rojo was rocked by a sharp pain in the head. She staggered, dazed and bewildered. What was happening to her?

'Listen to me, whoever you are,' a chilling voice spoke inside her mind.

'Where are you?' Rojo gasped. 'Who are you? And how did you get in my head?'

'No questions!' commanded the voice. 'You are here to serve me!'

Rojo tried to move away, but the pain

struck again. She fell to her knees. Suddenly, it seemed to her as if she were falling helplessly through a dark void. She saw a hideous squid-like face before her – except this squid was the size of a house and had glowing red eyes.

'You now possess power you could never have imagined,' the monster said. 'But, unless you find a way to use it, it will be worthless. Fulfil my demand and I will teach you. Fail me, and I will turn you to dust.'

'So what do you want?' asked Rojo. She could see she didn't exactly have a choice here.

'Only one thing,' the alien creature replied. 'A piece of valuable technology missing from my possession. And luckily you are already programmed to find it.'

The hospital ward was quiet. Grandpa lay in bed with his bandaged leg raised up, sleeping quietly. Ben and Gwen sat together by his bedside.

'Ben, you heard the doctor,' Gwen said. 'He's going to be fine. He's *Grandpa*.'

'I'm worried about him,' Ben sighed. Gwen's green eyes twinkled with mischief.

'I'd worry more about how some girl kicked Four Arms's butt,' she teased.

'Hey, heroes don't hit girls!' Ben protested.

'Good to know,' smiled Gwen, and smacked Ben in the arm with her fist. In a flash, Ben smacked her back.

'Ow!' cried Gwen. 'I thought you said –'

Ben interrupted her. 'I'm not in "hero" mode,' he explained. Then he fell silent again. He walked into the outside corridor and stared sadly out of the window.

'You OK?' Gwen asked. 'Normally, slugging me in the arm would make you feel much better!' Ben ignored her. He had started to study the dial of his Omnitrix watch.

'You know, what if I went Upgrade?' he wondered, remembering that that particular alien form that could enter machines and morph them into new, improved ones. 'I could get inside those machines he's hooked up to and see if I could make him better.'

'Ben, that won't work.'

'OK then,' Ben persisted. 'What if I went Ghostfreak? I could meld with him or something. I don't know. I just want to help him, you know?' Again, Ben clicked his watch thoughtfully. This time the central dial popped up, and green energy flashed.

It was enough. The power of the Omnitrix instantly registered in Rojo's brain. She'd been flying over the city, sensors primed for a moment like this. Her drone circuits lit up, sending messages through her upgraded body.

Now Rojo had just one purpose.

She swooped down on the hospital,

her sense-globes zeroing in on the shape of a schoolboy glimpsed through an upper-ward window. Her face lit up with a nasty smile.

'*There* you are!'

'Just relax,' Gwen said, trying to cheer Ben up. They were hanging out in the hospital corridor, just outside Grandpa's room. It was obvious Ben was still pretty upset. 'Everything's going to be OK,' she added brightly. Suddenly, she stood up, her eyes wide with shock.

SMASH! The next moment, Rojo crashed through the window, sending shards of glass flying everywhere. She landed like a big, dark bird of prey.

'Give me the Omnitrix!' she ordered. Ben and Gwen made a run for it.

'You want it? Come and get it!' Ben

taunted. They rounded the corner, dodging and weaving through nurses and porters. Rojo fired her lasers after them, not caring who she hit. One blast tore into a hospital trolley, destroying it in a burst of flames. Hospital staff scrambled for their lives.

'The stairs!' shouted Ben, spotting a nearby stairwell. They raced for the bottom as fast as they could, hoping their foe wouldn't guess where they had gone.

'Ben,' Gwen said, suddenly putting two and two together, 'that *thing* is the girl from the armoured car robbery! It's like she merged with those –'

'Robot drones!' completed Ben.

Suddenly, Rojo appeared at the top of the stairwell. She didn't use the steps. With one incredible, machine-powered leap, she jumped straight to the ground floor, landing where Ben and Gwen had passed only seconds before.

Laser blasts blew chunks out of a door

frame as they dashed out of the hospital into an ambulance park.

'OK, radical thought, but now might be a good time to go hero!' Gwen suggested.

To gain time, Ben ducked behind a row of old ambulances. Gwen followed. A moment later, Rojo was on the scene. She surveyed the row of vehicles. It was pretty clear her enemy was hiding, but she didn't plan on wasting time searching behind every ambulance.

'We can do this the easy way, or the hard way,' she said. Her laser beams targeted the rocky canyon walls above the hospital. Everything was about to change for the ancient boulders that had been lying up there sunning themselves peacefully for centuries. The laser ripped into the rock face and a great landslide headed towards the hospital.

From behind an ambulance, Ben spotted the danger unfolding. He clicked the watch's dial, selecting the powerful shape of Four Arms.

BLEEP! There was a burst of light and there stood Heatblast. The alien hero towered above Gwen, his white-hot body glowing inside a very cool red costume.

'Great. I need muscle and I get an alien candle instead,' groaned Heatblast. The rockslide was getting nearer. There were enough boulders there to pound the hospital into dust.

'If scissors cut paper, fire melts rock, right?' Heatblast raised his glowing hands and unleashed a burst of red-hot flame at the approaching boulders. **WHOOSH!** The rocks caught fire. Now *flaming* boulders were bouncing towards the hospital.

'OK,' admitted Heatblast. 'Definitely not what I had in mind.' He turned to Gwen. 'Go!' he yelled. Now was the time for drastic action. Heatblast zapped each ambulance in turn, and they all sagged together to form a wall of gooey metal. When the boulders came hurtling down, the wall held them back.

'Hospital's safe,' said Heatblast.

'But there are people at the bottom of that canyon!' Gwen cried out. Runaway rocks were still rumbling towards the city below.

'Oh, man, I hate it when you're right!' Heatblast moaned. He sped off after the boulders, but he didn't get far. Rojo streaked down from out of the sky to attack him from behind. She kicked Heatblast sprawling into the dust. Then Rojo powered up her lasers for a close-range attack. But Heatblast beat her to the punch: without a thought, he released a burst of solar fire, blasting her away.

He couldn't worry about his enemy now – he had boulders to catch. Heatblast leaped down the almost vertical wall of the canyon, surfing down the steep slope on a wave of fire. Far below, workmen fixing the road gazed up at the wall of rock hurtling towards them. It only had to cross the river bridge and it would be right on them. They ran, screaming, but there seemed little hope of escape.

SHROOOM! Heatblast unleashed white-hot flames that melted a hole in the great concrete bridge. A smoking chasm opened to welcome the tumbling boulders. One by one, they plunged harmlessly down into the water.

As Heatblast was admiring his work, Rojo flew down and grabbed him in her metal talons. Before he could fight back, she hurled him straight into the back of a dumper truck on a building site below. This time Rojo didn't plan on giving her enemy a chance.

POW, POW, POW! She unleashed one deadly ray blast after another, destroying the truck, the ground it stood on and everything else nearby. Even then she kept on firing into the smoke and flames that had engulfed the site below over and over again.

Finally, she stopped and smiled at the scene of utter devastation she'd caused. Then

the smirk disappeared off her half-robot face as she heard a rumbling underground. Rock flew into the air as Heatblast emerged from a smoking crater. He'd tunnelled away from her onslaught and was back – raring to fight.

'You want me?' he cried out. 'I'm right here!'

Recklessly, an enraged Rojo flew at him. Heatblast ducked out of the way and his opponent almost crashed into a wrecked fuel tanker lying in the road. Heatblast finally had

Rojo where he wanted her.

The fiery hero casually tossed a tiny little spark to the floor. It landed in a trail of fuel oil that had spilled from a crack in the tanker.

'See ya!' said Heatblast. A river of fire snaked from where he was standing, straight to the oil tanker behind his foe.

KA-BOOM! Rojo took the full force of the explosion. Meanwhile, Heatblast took off. That crazy robot lady wouldn't be bothering anybody for a while.

Moments later, Ben was back in the hospital checking up on Grandpa. He was awake again, still bandaged and sticking-plastered, but sitting up and keen to get his teeth into Ben's latest problem.

'When I was playing with my watch,' Ben said, 'I must've led her right to you.' He felt bad about being attacked right outside Grandpa's room. Not exactly the peace and quiet needed to recover.

'Since they've moved me to a new room and you haven't gone alien since then, we're safe,' Grandpa Max reasoned.

'Yeah, for now. But what about tomorrow?' Ben said, looking anxious. 'It's getting way too dangerous for you guys to be around me. If I didn't have this watch, none of this weird stuff would be happening.'

'Yeah, but since it won't come off, there's nothing we can do about it,' pointed out Gwen. Ben was gazing off into the distance, still unhappy.

'Maybe – maybe not,' he said, mysteriously. Ben was planning something he daren't tell either of them about.

Screaming crowds fled the scene as Rojo stomped through the centre of town. She'd recovered from the impact of the exploding fuel tanker and was back on the warpath, her red eyes scanning the horizon for any sign of her target. Then, suddenly, she was jolted by a surge of power in her mind. Vilgax was making contact again. In the blink of an eye, Rojo felt as though she were floating in a weird unknown realm, face to face with the sinister alien.

'The Omnitrix!' Vilgax shouted. 'Where is it?' But Rojo was more angry than scared this time round.

'I couldn't get it,' she snapped back. 'And

how nice you didn't tell me I'd be fighting a superhero! I'm through!'

She knew she wasn't really though. This game would only be over when Vilgax was through with her. A shock of pain shot through her half-robot body. Then she felt herself tumbling through endless darkness.

'You'll get me the Omnitrix,' Vilgax growled. 'And, if you fail again, your meaningless criminal life will be over. Now, this time, make him come to you.'

The hospital ward was silent, except for the soft breathing of Grandpa Max, still lying in his bed, and Gwen, who had fallen asleep in the chair by his side. Quietly, Ben placed a note on the bedside table. He took a final look at the two special people who had stood by him through all his troubles.

'I'm doing this for you, Grandpa,' Ben whispered, although he knew his grandfather couldn't hear him. Then he walked softly out of the room, alone.

Ben sat on the park bench, far away from the hospital. It was a sunny, peaceful afternoon. Over on the grass he saw a couple of people having fun – a boy throwing a football around with his grey-haired grandfather.

'I'm glad we can spend summer together, Grandpa,' the kid said. Ben looked sad. That was how life should be – how his life would never be. Nearby, a lady was sitting in the sun listening to her radio. Then the local news report came on and Ben's ears pricked up.

'Reports say the armoured attacker had incredible fire power and has blown up several police road blocks before arriving at the Police Academy Training Centre just outside of the city . . .'

Ben instantly knew what he had to do.

The blue shadows of late afternoon had crept across the hospital ward. Gwen suddenly woke up with a start and realised that Ben had gone. She spotted his note and read it straight away.

'Dear Grandpa and Gwen,' she read aloud. 'I care about you both too much to keep putting you in danger. It's better this way. Love, Ben.'

Grandpa Max woke up and saw Gwen sitting there with a sad look on her face.

'Gwen, what is it?' he asked. They glanced up to the TV above, to the news report that was in progress. Gwen turned up the volume with the remote.

'The attack at the police training centre continues,' a voice announced. Pictures flashed across the screen of fire, smoke and the ruthless figure of Rojo, blazing a trail of destruction. 'Early reports say several officers have been injured.'

Gwen was in no doubt about where her cousin had sneaked off.

'Ben's gone,' she replied. 'But I think I know where he went. I've got to go, Grandpa.'

'I'm coming too,' said Grandpa Max. He strained all his muscles, but his body would not respond.

'You can't go anywhere,' Gwen told him. He tried to struggle up again without success.

'You can't go alone. It's too dangerous,' Grandpa Max protested. Gwen picked up a small remote control unit and aimed it at the bed. With a swift click she raised the end of the bed a little higher.

'I can't get up now,' Grandpa Max groaned.

'That's the point!' said Gwen. She placed the remote unit on a shelf out of his reach and made her exit – deaf to all her grandfather's attempts to call her back.

Outside in the car park, two medics were hopping into the front seats of an ambulance.

'They need us down at the police academy,' one said. They were in such a hurry to get going that they didn't notice Gwen slipping into the back of the vehicle just before it pulled away.

They had no problem locating the trouble spot – the thick smoke was visible from right across town. Rojo stood in the street below, coolly admiring her own demolition job. She swept her lasers across the building again, ripping its stonework apart.

Suddenly, Rojo was smashed off her feet. She looked up and saw a sleek alien form speeding away. It had a pointy black helmet, a stripy tail and whizzed around on weird, ball-like feet. XLR8 was in action!

'Looks like you got this party started without me!' XLR8 said, his bright-green eyes seeming to laugh at her from his neon-blue face.

XLR8 zoomed towards Rojo again, but this time she was ready for him. Stepping to one side, she grabbed him with a robotic claw and swung him on to the ground, then booted him straight into the back of a parked car.

'He wants his Omnitrix – he can have it!' grinned Rojo. 'This is getting fun.'

'Who's "he"?' asked XLR8, sounding a little dazed. Rojo loomed over him, lining up her

lasers to deal out the finishing blow. But XLR8 sprang up and launched a super-speed multiple body-kick at her, rocking her robotic form backwards with his fast-flying feet.

'One good kick deserves another!' he said as a final boot sent Rojo flying. XLR8 activated his visor, which slid down over his face. Now he was ready for anything his opponent could dish out.

A dull rumble made them both turn in surprise. They'd been too busy fighting to notice that the cops at the academy had decided it was time to defend themselves. The vast bulk of a heavily armoured tank lumbered into view, aiming its massive gun turret straight at them.

XLR8 knew what to do in situations like this – get the heck out of there. **KA-BOOM!** Rojo took the full blast of the cannon. XLR8 wheeled around to take stock of the situation.

Thick grey smoke billowed everywhere. Then out of the dark clouds rolled the tank, taking aim at XLR8. To his astonishment, the huge war-machine suddenly rose into the sky. Rojo was lifting it above her head! She was still in one piece, still sure of victory, still out to get the Omnitrix.

'Nice try!' she said, 'but "Speedy" is all mine!' The tank crew leaped to safety just in time, as Rojo hurled the massive vehicle at her foe. It exploded into the tarmac in a mass of mangled metal – but its target had long since disappeared.

XLR8 appeared behind Rojo and hit her with a series of swift punches – punches so fast she had no time to hit back. Once again, Rojo found herself on the ground. This time she had had enough. She knew her foe was too quick for her to beat in hand-to-hand combat, but she did have her deadly laser cannons. She unleashed a searing blast at XLR8, sending him skidding across the ground. This time, she had succeeded. Her enemy was dazed, maybe even out for the count.

An ambulance pulled up on the scene, the driver too blinded by the smoke and dust to see the danger he was heading into.

'Who needs help?' the medic called out. XLR8 sure did. Rojo had lifted him up, and was about to dash his body to the floor. At that moment, Gwen peeped out of the ambulance door, trying to spot her cousin.

XLR8 stirred to life and spotted Gwen – right in the middle of the combat zone. Like a streak of light, he zipped out of Rojo's grip and whisked Gwen away from the scene. Moments later, they were in a nearby alley.

'What are you doing here?' XLR8 asked, amazed.

'It's better this way,' Gwen said, with feeling. 'Sound familiar?' Ben realised she was quoting his goodbye note. Then the cousins heard a high-pitched sound they recognised only too well.

'So does that bleeping,' said XLR8. In a flash of red energy, he morphed back into a ten-year-old boy.

'Uh. Just great,' Ben said sarcastically. Rojo could now be heard, blasting her way towards them. 'Come on!' Ben said.

Ducking and weaving to avoid the volley of explosions from behind them, the Tennysons raced into the academy's shooting range and hid behind a human-shaped target.

'Ben, you can't run away from us,' Gwen said.

'Don't tell me what I can or can't do!' Ben whispered back. 'This is *my* fight – *my* weird watch not yours.' As they spoke, an angry Rojo was scanning the area, shooting up the target range as it had never been blasted before.

'Yeah,' replied Gwen, about as sincere as Ben had ever heard her, 'but you're *my* weird cousin.'

BLAM, BLAM, BLAM! Rojo was taking apart the target range, piece by piece. Soon there would be nowhere left to hide.

'In here!' Gwen hissed. The two cousins raced through a side door into the gymnasium. They looked around for a new hiding place among all the workout machines, balls and weights. In the middle of all the excitement, Gwen's phone rang. Guessing who was on the line, she took the call – and quickly handed it over to Ben.

'It's for you,' she said. Ben looked puzzled.

'Hello?' He couldn't help wondering who on Earth could be calling him at a time like this. Then he cringed, frowned and glared at Gwen. She had put him through to Grandpa Max.

'Can we talk later?' Ben asked. 'I've got an indestructible robot-thing none of my aliens can take out on my tail!'

Back in the hospital, Grandpa Max was on the road to recovery. He was sitting up in bed, clear-eyed, that old determined look on his face.

He spoke urgently into his mobile phone.

'Ben, if you can't destroy it from the outside, take it down from the inside.'

Ben's eyes lit up. He realised exactly what Grandpa Max was driving at.

'That's it!' he cried out. 'Thanks!' He flipped the phone shut and handed it to Gwen. She had that familiar sparkle in her big green eyes.

'Looks like *you're* not better off without Grandpa, huh?'

Outside, Rojo was closing in. Her prey had somehow escaped her so far, but her drone computers told her there was only one place left for her foe to hide. She flew towards the gym.

Inside, Ben was crouching behind a pillar, clicking the dial on his Omnitrix. As usual, it wasn't playing ball. **THWACK!** Ben started to thump the dial, with increasing urgency. Yesss! He'd finally done it! In a blinding flash, a big, flowing shape rose up in place of the ten-year-old boy. It had a circular face and flashing green circuits dotted about its black-and-white body. Upgrade was ready to go to work!

CRASH! Rojo made a surprise entrance through the roof, enjoying the destruction she was causing. She floated through the silent gym, scanning for her target. She didn't see Gwen cowering behind a weights machine, and she certainly didn't see Upgrade spread out across the ceiling like an enormous high-tech pancake.

FLUMP! Down Ben fell, covering Rojo's head and sinking into her armour, invading her computer systems. Upgrade could enter, explore and improve any device. He could also wreck anything.

'Agghh!' Rojo cried out in pain. For the first time in the whole battle she realised she was in big trouble. Upgrade was breaking down Rojo's defences, preparing to disable her weapons, shut down her computers, make her useless.

Suddenly, Upgrade clutched at his head, crying out in pain. He'd entered Rojo's computer mind – a brain programmed to make contact with Vilgax. Ben was about to come face to face with his deadliest enemy.

CHAPTER SIX

SHUT DOWN

Upgrade felt like he was floating through dark space, away from everything he knew, unable to fight back. Before him was an enormous squid-like head, its creepy red eyes burning into him. He was being held by an alien claw, as if he were just a toy.

'Listen to every word,' said a cold alien voice. 'Be afraid. You cannot run, you cannot hide from me. I will find you. And, when I do, I will retrieve my Omnitrix and destroy you!'

Suddenly, Vilgax disappeared. The link between their minds was broken. Rojo began to struggle. She jerked her head back and threw Upgrade off her. The big, floppy alien hit a concrete pillar and slid down it.

Upgrade was out of Rojo's system, but by no means out of the fight. He quickly melded with an exercise machine, reached out with his metal handles and grabbed Rojo's head, beating it against his own solid frame.

'Time to work out!' Upgrade said as Rojo fell on to a treadmill machine. Upgrade swiftly melded with that, and sped up the walking belt to catapult Rojo head first into another machine. **WHAM!** She was on the ropes at last.

A groggy Rojo stumbled away just as a team of police marksmen entered the gym. They were all wearing protective masks and carrying the latest high-tech laser rifles.

'Duck!' screamed Gwen, who was the first to spot them. **BLAM, BLAM, BLAM!** – the cops were in no mood to take prisoners. Blast after blast rocked Rojo's armoured body. While she was distracted, Upgrade leaped at her for a final time, covering her like a wad of soft bubblegum.

'Now, this won't hurt a bit,' he said, seeping into each and every one of her circuits.

'Aaggh!' cried Rojo. 'Get out of me!'

Upgrade invaded her systems at lightning speed, did as much damage as he could, and then ejected himself straight out again.

'OK, I lied,' he said, leaving Rojo a shattered, quivering wreck.

The police team stood back, weapons at the ready. But they needn't have bothered – Rojo would never attack anyone again. She cracked, she shook, she wobbled and then she fell to bits.

One by one, her drone implants flew off and crashed to the ground. Her body was restored to its original form. Even the energy blaster she had used in the robbery earlier in the day returned to its original shape and clattered to the ground.

'I-I'm normal,' she moaned, still in a daze. Her clothes were a little ragged, her pride a little dented, but she was back in one piece, and as full of bad attitude as ever.

'Abnormal's way more like it,' commented

Upgrade. Joey had spotted her weapon and was already edging her way towards it.

'Look, I don't know what came over me,' she said in a pathetic, put-on voice. 'Please, you've got to help me. I'm just a girl.' As Upgrade hesitated, Joey snatched up her gun and aimed it at him.

'Guess what?' came a voice behind her. It was Gwen, flying straight at Joey, with her best *tae kwon do* kick. 'So am I!'

Joey crashed back into a pillar, and the whole gym began to shudder and crumble to the floor.

'Gwen, we've got to go!' shouted Upgrade as the place started to come down around their ears. Gwen and the police team fled, but Upgrade bent down and picked up the unconscious Joey and carried her out.

'She's all yours,' Upgrade said, in true hero style, and handed the defeated Joey over to the cops.

Night had fallen. Upgrade and Gwen tasted the cool air and stood side by side under the starlit sky. The end of another adventure always tasted sweet.

A few minutes later, the Tennysons were reunited. The Rust Bucket was standing in the hospital car park, and lumbering towards it was a big, grey-haired guy, in a bright red tropical shirt, on a pair of crutches.

'It's good to get out of here and get back on the road,' said Grandpa Max. But Gwen still had an unanswered question.

'So, Ben, what happened back there in the gym? It's like you were possessed or something.'

'I don't know,' Ben replied. 'It was like when I went Upgrade I saw this alien. We were both floating through space and he was talking to me. It looked kind of like he had this octopus on his head. He said I should be afraid.'

His grandfather frowned. The description of the weird vision had obviously bothered him.

'Grandpa,' Ben said. 'You look worried.'

'I'm fine,' said Grandpa Max, hiding his true feelings. 'You'll be fine too. As long as we stay together.' Ben smiled, remembering the note he had left them just hours before. From now on, walking away from his family was no longer an option.

'Sounds good to me,' he said.

Grandpa Max stared up at the twinkling stars. They looked beautiful. But he knew that somewhere up there, a pair of evil red eyes was looking right back down at the Earth – forever hunting the Omnitrix.

BEN, GWEN AND GRANDPA FACE A TRIO OF ROBBERS

FOUR ARMS COMES DOWN HARD ON THE GANG

ROBBER JOEY MUTATES INTO
HALF ROBOT 'ROJO'!

SHE AND HEATBLAST GO HEAD TO HEAD

WHILE POOR GRANDPA MAX IS LAID UP IN BED

ROJO CAN'T GET UPGRADE OFF HER MIND

THEN THE PLAN BACKFIRES WHEN
VILGAX TAKES CONTROL

BUT GOOD TRIUMPHS AND
THE TENNYSONS HIT THE ROAD

BEN RISKS UPGRADE-ING, DESPITE THE THREAT OF VILGAX

EVIL DRONES FOLLOW THE OMNITRIX SIGNAL TO TOWN

VILGAX FINALLY GETS BEN IN HIS SIGHTS

BUT GRANDPA MAX COMES TO THE RESCUE!

FOUR ARMS PUTS A FIST IN THE WORKS OF VILGAX'S PLAN

AND DIAMONDHEAD TAKES AIM AT HIS EVIL ENEMY

BUT IT LOOKS LIKE VILGAX HAS THE UPPER CLAW

UNTIL BEN MAKES SURE HE GOES OUT WITH A BANG!

BEN 10™
SECRETS

It was the big news story of the day.

'We're live on the scene of a high-speed police pursuit,' the TV reporter announced to shocked viewers across the nation. 'An armoured car full of gold has been stolen and the thieves are now making their getaway. It is believed the thieves also have a hostage!' he added.

It looked bad. The robbers were driving like madmen; pretty soon there would be a massive pile-up on the highway as traffic scrambled to get out of the way of the chase.

Then it happened. Something unexpected. Something totally cool.

Sharp green crystals sprang right up out of the road and ripped into the tyres of the armoured car. Out of control, it spun into the guard rail at the side of the highway.

The police squad cars pulled up, surrounding the stolen car. A shaven-headed thief in high-tech goggles jumped out, dragging the frightened hostage with him. A second member of the gang appeared, carrying an enormous laser cannon.

ZAP! A blast like forked lightning blew one of the squad cars clean off the ground.

'Wait! What's this?' gasped the excited voice of the news reporter. Behind the armed thief, emerging out of the smoke and dust, an incredible figure appeared: a giant being of ice-green crystal.

The thief whirled round, only to see his laser cannon sliced to pieces by a glinting green claw. The robber turned to run, but was lifted up by a huge, fast-growing crystal that sprouted out of the ground and left him dangling helplessly in the air.

'Yes,' said the thrilled news reporter. 'It looks like we have another alien sighting.'

But this was no alien. It was just a regular, ten-year-old human boy. Benjamin Tennyson. And today Ben had morphed into the awesome form of Diamondhead.

The remaining robber gazed up at the green giant who blocked his way. He formed an instant, very sensible plan: he gave up.

'We don't know where these strange creatures come from, but they seem to be here to help,' the news reporter concluded. Diamondhead grinned. The cops moved in – it was all over.

Not everyone watching had enjoyed the show. Far out in space, a pair of evil red eyes had seen everything. Vilgax had followed the whole chase on the wall-sized viewing screens in his space ship.

'The Omnitrix – wasted on pointless heroics!' he growled. A small robot looked up, eager to help.

'Shall I send more drones to get it?'

There was a hiss of steam as the doors of the recovery pod opened and the alien strode out. Vilgax was ready to rumble. This evil being was so tall he almost made a hero like Diamondhead look like a toy action figure. He had the face of a sly space-squid, perched on top of a giant body encased in gleaming armour.

'No,' replied Vilgax. 'I will see to this task myself.'

'Ugh!' Ben sat up in the dark, wild-eyed and afraid. He was relieved to realise that he was

safe and sound in The Rust Bucket – the big motorhome owned by his grandpa, Max.

'Another nightmare, Ben?' asked his grandfather, swiftly arriving at the side of Ben's bunk.

'It was that weird alien from my vision,' Ben said, remembering a previous adventure when the same creepy face had appeared in his mind. 'Only this one was bigger, uglier and scarier,' he added.

Ben's cousin Gwen rolled over in the bunk

below him. Her bright-green eyes flashed with annoyance at being woken up.

'Sure you weren't just looking in a mirror?' she asked. Grandpa Max gave a tired smile.

'It was just a bad dream, son,' he said. 'We can talk about it in the morning.' But Ben was still shaken by his nightmare.

'He looked right at me,' Ben protested, 'and he said, "I'm coming for you now!"'

Grandpa Max froze in his tracks. Then, as calmly as he could, he made straight for the driver's seat.

'Change of plan,' he said grimly. 'We're hitting the road right now.'

Gwen groaned. 'It's three in the morning!'

The huge six-wheeler rumbled into life and swung out on to the deserted highway.

'Best way to beat the traffic,' said Grandpa.

The sun was shining down on the plains of South Dakota, and curious bison turned their shaggy heads to watch The Rust Bucket roar through their land. It was half a day later, and the Tennysons were nearing their destination.

'I want to make Mount Rushmore by nightfall,' Grandpa Max explained, to fend off yet another question about his need for speed. Ben was bored. He and Gwen had spent countless hours on the road that summer on their endless camping trip. Now, just watching Grandpa scaring the wildlife with his driving was getting a bit old.

'Let me play a game,' Ben begged, watching Gwen at her laptop computer.

'I would,' Gwen said sweetly, 'but I think this will be a good lesson for you to learn how to entertain yourself.'

Ben looked glum. Then he grinned a fiendish grin. He knew how to entertain himself all right. He checked the dial on his Omnitrix, and clicked it into life.

* * *

At exactly that moment, orbiting the Earth, Vilgax stirred in his command chair. His monitor systems had just gone wild.

'The Omnitrix has been activated. Pinpoint its location!'

A holographic map of the Earth spun before Vilgax, until it zeroed in on its target: South Dakota, North America. Vilgax smiled.

'I have you now!'

Gwen was puzzled, not to mention annoyed. Her computer had suddenly gone crazy; she couldn't make it do a thing. Now the screen had gone black, suggesting total power failure.

'Hey, what gives?' A green stick-man appeared on the monitor.

'Sorry,' its robotic voice informed her, 'you are a loser.' Gwen looked astonished.

'And you always will be!' giggled Ben, who had invaded the computer as Upgrade, his high-tech alien form.

'Get out of my computer!' shouted Gwen. Her laptop had now sprouted legs, and scuttled away from her like a bug.

'What? I'm just entertaining myself,' teased Ben. 'Oooh, what's this? A diary?' he added. Now things were getting interesting! '"Dear Diary,"' Upgrade read, '"my cousin Ben is such a –"'

'Doofus!' Gwen exploded. 'Knock it off!' Grandpa Max turned and snapped at Ben.

'Now is not the time to go alien! Do you understand?' he shouted. Upgrade oozed sadly out of the computer.

'I was just fooling around,' the floppy

creature sighed, the pale circle of his face blinking glumly. 'What kind of attention could I attract in here?'

In a flash, Upgrade changed back to Ben.

'Never mind,' muttered Grandpa Max.

Ben and Gwen exchanged puzzled looks. Grandpa really was in a weird mood.

Unknown to the crew of The Rust Bucket, Vilgax's gleaming ship was poised, far out in space, directly above them.

'We've lost the Omnitrix signal,' came the report. Vilgax peered down on his robotic second-in-command.

'No matter,' Vilgax replied. 'I've narrowed down its location.' The sinister alien turned his tentacled head to gaze at his monitors. They showed images of Ben in his various forms, rescuing people from every kind of peril.

'I know just how to draw this Earthling out.'

Moments later, a great dark shadow fell across the prairies of South Dakota as Vilgax's ship lowered itself to land. A hatch hissed open and out rolled a huge spiked metal ball. Deadly flying probes – robot drones – buzzed alongside like big angry hornets.

A friendly sign greeted the alien visitors: Welcome to Rapid City. The drones zapped it to bits, while the spiked ball rolled on towards the sleepy city.

Screams filled the air as the alien demolition force struck in the heart of downtown Rapid City. The spiked ball powered through the side of an office block, chewing through its concrete walls as if they were soggy cardboard. The drones darted here and there, their deadly lasers destroying parked cars.

KA-BOOM! The central petrol station went up in a sheet of orange flame, a jet-black cloud mushrooming out across the city.

‘What’s going on over there?’ Ben gaped out of the window of the speeding Rust Bucket at the smoke rising up into the blue sky.

‘I’m sure the authorities have the situation well in hand,’ remarked Grandpa Max, not seeming at all interested. For once, Ben thought his grandfather had called it wrong.

‘Looks like it’s hero time!’

He checked out the dial on the Omnitrix, clicking through the selection of forms, until he hit the right one. Grandpa Max shot him an anxious glance.

‘Ben, I don’t think that’s the best idea –’

Too late – Ben had made his mind up. He braced himself to face the surge of power, as his cells morphed like wildfire across his whole body.

‘Time to turn up the Heatblast on these guys!’ The Rust Bucket door flew open and out shot Heatblast himself, his hands glowing like coals, his head a ball of flame, the round Omnitrix symbol displayed on the chest of his red-and-white costume.

'Hey,' he shouted, 'why don't you pick on someone with real firepower?'

The drones didn't know what hit them. Red-hot fireballs blasted them out of the sky, melted their weapons and left them lying in pools of molten metal. Heatblast was having a ball. It wasn't often he got to let rip like this.

But now the fun part was over. Heatblast realised he had been tricked. Hunting his foes, he had been lured into the centre of a whole swarm of angry drones. They hovered around him silently, ready to strike.

'Oh, man, I didn't mean all at once!' he groaned. The drones moved in closer, their weapons crackling with power as they charged up.

'Why do I get the feeling you were expecting me?' Heatblast wondered out loud. Then he leaped into action – spinning in a circle he fired a scorching blast of flame, melting the drone ships one by one, until they all slumped to the ground in a great ring of bubbling metal.

That was when things turned serious. Heatblast was suddenly pinned to a wall by four metal probes that shot at him out of nowhere, ensnaring him in their beams of power. Heatblast was well and truly trapped! He watched, helpless, as a massive spiked ball rolled towards him.

It rumbled to a halt. A hatch opened. An enormous figure emerged, its heavy feet shattering the sidewalk. Vilgax loomed above Heatblast, his narrow red eyes squinting down at his captive.

'You!' gasped Heatblast. 'You're the alien from my visions!'

'At last we meet,' the monstrous creature snarled. 'The being that has caused me so much trouble.'

Rapid City was a smoking inferno. Trapped in the middle was Heatblast, and inside Heatblast was Ben. He knew he was facing the battle of his life.

'Who are you?' Heatblast asked.

'I am Vilgax and I have come for the Omnitrix,' rasped an unearthly voice. Ben

needed to play for time while he figured out a way to escape.

'And, uh, I'm guessing you're not with the good guys,' Heatblast said. He knew action spoke louder than small talk at a time like this so, with a sudden effort, he turned up his body heat, melting the devices holding him and tearing himself free of the wall.

Now it was payback time! Heatblast launched an all-out attack on Vilgax, dealing out blow after blow with his fists of fire. Something made him stop and look up; he was punching the giant alien in the ankle and having absolutely zero effect.

Vilgax grabbed Heatblast viciously, swung him back, then hurled him through five tower blocks. It may have been six – Ben found it hard to keep track of the exact number. Heatblast pulled himself up out of the smoking crater where he had finally wound up, and looked worried.

'OK,' he sighed, 'this guy's really tough.'

There was no let-up with this creep. Vilgax was now bounding across town, straight towards Heatblast, at incredible speed.

'I've got to slow him down,' Heatblast told himself. It was time to use his head. Instead of aiming his firepower straight at the alien, he targeted the road in front of him. It smoked, bubbled and melted into a swamp of sticky black tar.

Vilgax's massive feet got stuck in the molten gloop, causing him to topple over like

a falling tree. He landed with a satisfying **SHLOCK** in the hot goo, and struggled to escape.

Right then, The Rust Bucket turned up on the scene. Grandpa Max stared at the fallen Vilgax in disbelief.

'No!' he gasped. 'It can't be!' He put his foot down on the accelerator and screeched towards Heatblast. Gwen threw the door open.

'Grandpa says to get in,' she said. 'Now.'

Heatblast wasn't so sure. He thought he finally had Mr Squid-head where he wanted him.

'I'm just about to kick alien butt!' he protested. **BLEEP!** Heatblast heard the sound he dreaded most. The Omnitrix had decided that playtime was over; in a flash he morphed back into Ben.

The Rust Bucket pulled away – faster than Ben could ever remember it doing before.

'Believe me when I say you do not want to pick a fight with Vilgax,' Grandpa Max said. Ben frowned. One little question sprang to mind.

'Uhhh, how do you know his name is Vilgax?'

Gwen was starting to lose her cool. 'Grandpa, what aren't you telling us?'

Before Grandpa Max could reply, a sudden blast rocked the vehicle from side to side. Gwen whirled round to check the rear view.

'Two robot goons, closing in fast!'

Grandpa Max looked grim. It was time for some serious getaway driving.

'Hold on!' He swerved The Rust Bucket across three lanes of the deserted highway, dodging the energy blasts of the fast-approaching drones.

Again, the deadly craft swooped overhead, but Grandpa Max swung the wheel crazily to shake them off for a second time. He was pleased that he had at least drawn the drones away from other traffic. No more innocent bystanders were going to get caught up in this battle.

BLAM! The enemy was back, its fireballs landing closer than ever. Hurled from side to side of the vehicle, Gwen was clinging on for dear life.

'We can't keep this up forever!' she warned. Grandpa Max stuck to the job. He would keep it up forever if he had to.

'Things are going to get a whole lot

worse if we don't get to Mount Rushmore,' he remarked. Ben was fiddling with the dial of his watch, trying to coax it into giving him another form – fast. Meanwhile, Gwen was close to freaking out.

'Why?' she cried out. 'What's at Mount Rushmore?' Grandpa Max didn't have time to explain.

'You're going to have to trust me,' he said. **THUD!** A sudden impact rocked The Rust Bucket. Something had landed on the roof.

'Well, I'm not going down without a fight!' Ben promised. He'd finally done it. With a grin of delight, he lined up the rings on the watch and a winged figure appeared on the dial. There was a bright glow and there, instead of Ben, was Stinkfly.

'Yes!' The six-legged, four-horned alien bug hovered on its jagged wings and shot out of the door.

'Ben! Wait!' Grandpa Max called.

But Stinkfly wasn't planning on hanging around. For starters, he had to dodge the attacks of those nasty little flying pests. Then he wheeled around in the air, opened his jaws and spewed out a great spinning glob of stink-slime. **POW!** It exploded, taking down a pair of drones with it.

But one of his pursuers had escaped the blast. Stinkfly latched on to the back of the final drone and sliced through its rear section with his diamond-shaped tail. The drone plunged to the ground and exploded in a cloud of smoke. Stinkfly circled the scene of his triumph with glee.

'Floats like a butterfly, stings like a Stinkfly!' he boasted in a voice like the whine of a mosquito. But he hadn't spotted the weird cocoon beneath him. Stinkfly had just flown back over the place where he had just left Vilgax.

The gigantic alien, revived and ready for

action after his spell in the cocoon, ripped his way out of his glowing red shell, sprang up and grabbed on to one of Stinkfly's many legs.

'Give me the Omnitrix!' demanded Vilgax. Stinkfly swooped and soared but his enemy clung on tight.

'Who is this guy?' Stinkfly wondered aloud. He summoned up a massive ooze-attack and squirted Vilgax with a flood of the vilest goo he had. The big alien was forced to let go and crashed to the ground.

The Rust Bucket, no longer under attack, came to a halt. The dust from Vilgax's fall was starting to clear, and Grandpa Max could finally study the scene and assess the situation. He suddenly put his foot hard down on the accelerator and sped away from the action.

'Where are we going?' asked Gwen in surprise, now seated up front with Grandpa Max. 'We have to help Ben!'

'We will,' said Grandpa Max at the wheel. 'But first we'll need to get some special help.'

'Let me guess – at Mount Rushmore,' Gwen suggested. Grandpa Max said nothing, but drove on like a man with a mission.

'Grandpa, you're really freaking me out,' Gwen added. She had never seen her grandfather like this before, and she realised they were probably facing their biggest crisis yet.

Grandpa Max and Gwen had left the scene of Vilgax's fall just in time. The evil alien, now fully recovered, had climbed back to his feet and was madder than ever. He stomped off in pursuit of his prey. Vilgax couldn't fly, but he bounded across the city, from rooftop to rooftop, leaving a trail of crushed office blocks behind him, like broken sandcastles.

Stinkfly hovered on the edge of the city, away from any high buildings, but he still he wasn't safe. With a final incredible bound, Vilgax snatched him out of the sky. Stinkfly was like a little bug in the alien's huge claw. As far as Vilgax was concerned, it was game over.

'I grow tired of this,' he muttered, and, showing surprising skill for a towering alien menace, he lightly touched the centre of the Omnitrix with the tip of his horny claw. There was a **BLEEP!** and suddenly Ben was hanging there helpless.

'Hey, how'd you do that?' Ben complained. Vilgax gazed at the ten-year-old Earth boy with surprise, fury and disgust.

'A child?' he roared. 'The Omnitrix is in

the hands of a mere child?'

Vilgax tried to remove the device, but it unleashed a massive shock, blasting the alien head-over-tentacles into a wall. Ben tried to scuttle away and lose himself in the rubble, but his enemy had grabbed him again in seconds.

'It appears the Omnitrix has already merged with your own DNA,' Vilgax said.

'I, uh, don't suppose that means you're going to let me go, does it?' Ben asked hopefully.

'Hardly,' came the cold reply. Vilgax's landing craft, the great spiked ball, rolled up. The alien tossed Ben inside, then climbed in after him. The door slammed shut, and the ball rumbled away.

Rising up from the plains of South Dakota, Mount Rushmore loomed before them. The great stone faces of four presidents, carved into the mighty rock, gazed down as The Rust Bucket roared up the winding track into the heart of the hills. Gwen glanced around, nervous.

'I don't think tourists are allowed on this road,' she said. Grandpa shook his head with a knowing smile.

'We're not tourists,' he said. 'We're tenants.' He brought The Rust Bucket to a stop at a remote spot next to a sign saying 'road closed'. Then he hit a secret switch under the dashboard.

There was a grinding noise, a sudden jolt, then the sound of powerful machinery whirring into life. A large circular platform appeared under the vehicle and lowered it down into a hidden shaft.

Grandpa Max and Gwen were in a cavernous underground bunker, a secret base located behind the faces of those famous presidents of old. The whole place was deserted, as if abandoned many years ago. Gwen looked around with awe. She was gazing at row upon row of secret compartments. Grandpa Max, totally at home in this incredible place, pulled open one of the oversized drawers.

Inside was a weird device. Weird as in amazing – amazing as in seriously cool futuristic technology. Gwen had finally had enough.

'That's it!' she shouted, folding her arms. 'I'm not taking another step until you tell me what's going on!'

Grandpa Max swung round, holding the

biggest gun Gwen had ever seen in her life – and that included stuff she'd seen in movies. To operate the weapon, Grandpa Max was kitted up in a special visor. He pressed a switch to charge up the gun and blue energy crackled to life in a see-through tube.

'I wasn't exactly your normal plumber when I retired,' he said.

Ben was sure he must have been in tighter spots than this – but right now he couldn't quite remember any. He was trapped in the control room of Vilgax's spaceship, his left arm – the one attached to the Omnitrix – was swallowed up inside a gigantic clamp. His other limbs were held in beams of energy. On top of this, he was suspended high above the ground so that Vilgax could get a better look at him.

'A child,' Vilgax murmured, with hatred in his voice. 'I should've suspected as much.' Gigantic screens revealed every detail of Ben's biology, his DNA, the type, size and number of his every molecule. Another set of laser projections revealed the forms he had morphed into, including XLR8, the tiny alien Grey Matter and Four Arms.

'The Omnitrix being used as a plaything!' Vilgax snorted.

'Hey, I've saved a lot of people by going

hero!' Ben protested. The giant alien ignored him.

'You hold the key to a power struggle so ancient, so vast, it is beyond your comprehension,' Vilgax said. A holographic image appeared before Ben's eyes, as if it were beamed directly from the alien's mind, showing a terrible cosmic war; an incredible army defeating all before it. And every soldier in that army was a different one of Ben's forms. XLR8, Heatblast, Stinkfly, side by side in a ruthless attacking force.

'Picture an entire army,' Vilgax said, 'each in command of an Omnitrix – and all at my command! I will be invincible! I will rule the universe!'

Ben didn't like what he was seeing. He struggled helplessly against the weird device that held him aloft.

'And the only thing between me and my destiny is you,' Vilgax growled. Then a bank of

instruments rose up through the floor, bristling with probes, drills and an endless variety of gleaming blades.

The Rust Bucket was back on the road. Grandpa Max was now tearing back towards the scene of the action as fast as he had left it minutes before. Except now Grandpa believed he had the tools to do the job.

'This weapon,' he said, glancing at the outsized cannon he had removed from the secret base, 'is keyed into Vilgax's bio-signature. Hopefully, it'll take him down for good this time.' Gwen took a moment to let this sink in.

'This time?' she asked. Grandpa Max's eyes stayed on the road, which was being gobbled up at an incredible rate by the speeding motorhome.

'There's a small red button under that cabinet,' he told Gwen. 'Press it.'

Gwen did so. A secret compartment flipped open in the dashboard, revealing a high-tech, laser-display tracking system. To Gwen's increasing surprise, there was already a red dot bleeping on the map – revealing the location of Ben and the Omnitrix.

'GPS-assisted tracking system,' Grandpa Max said. 'It's locked on the watch's signal. You navigate.'

Back on the spaceship, Vilgax had selected the fiendish alien probe he wanted to use on his annoying human foe first. He chose a blade that looked to Ben like an outer-space tin-opener. The robotic servants bustled about checking the status of the ship's weapon systems. Countless tiny drones made the ship ready for departure.

'Prepare for take off!' Vilgax announced.

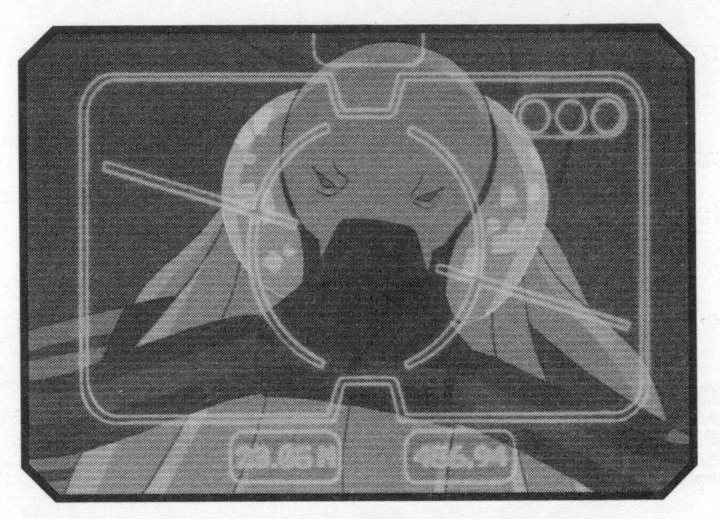

'Once we're in orbit, I will finally have the pleasure of destroying this miserable planet once and for all.' Vilgax raised his shimmering blade. Ben stared with terror.

'I'm going to enjoy this,' smiled Vilgax. The floor was shaking. The great spaceship was powering up its engines ready for lift off.

Gwen had always thought it would be kind of cool to go off-road in The Rust Bucket, but not quite like this. Grandpa Max, his jaw set in grim determination, was speeding downhill straight towards the alien craft. Gwen couldn't bear to look. Was he just going to crash right into it?

'We have to get aboard!' Grandpa Max said.

'Get aboard?' gasped Gwen. 'How?' Her grandfather grinned cheekily and, for a split second, Gwen was reminded of her cousin Ben's face when he was cooking up a surprise for her. Grandpa, it turned out, had another secret panel hidden away in his dashboard.

A massive, high-tech battering ram sprang from the front of The Rust Bucket. Gwen squeezed her eyes shut as they hit the side of the spaceship at full speed.

KA-BOOM! The impact shook the whole ship. Grandpa Max blasted the horn to announce his arrival. The Rust Bucket smashed through the outer hull, straight into the control centre, slamming right into Vilgax. The force of the crash carried the alien across the room and buried his body deep into the far wall.

'Warning! Hull breach! Power surge!' the robot drones reported, rushing about like headless chickens. It was too late to stop the vast ship from taking off, and it lurched into the sky, out of control.

The power surge in the command centre had lit up the Omnitrix. Sparks flashed in the air around Ben's wrist. Ben wriggled, desperately trying to escape from his bonds. Vilgax was back on his feet and bearing down on him again, determined to cut the precious device free.

'Claws off my grandson, Vilgax!' Grandpa Max appeared through the smoke, aiming his special weapon right at the alien.

'Grandpa!' Ben could hardly believe his eyes. Grandpa Max had suddenly, amazingly, turned into an all-action hero. Was it a dream?

'Tennyson!' Vilgax hissed, with a trace

of grudging respect. It was clear the two had history.

Right now, Grandpa Max had just one thing on his mind – bringing down the monster that dared to threaten his family.

BLAM! A streak of blue lightning blasted Vilgax straight through the wall of his control room. He crashed out of sight in a cloud of smoke. Ben could only stare, open-mouthed, at this new version of Grandpa Max – the alien-butt kicker!

'You know this guy?'

'It's a long story,' Grandpa Max replied. But before he could say any more, the Omnitrix started to go haywire. It pulsed with power, sending Ben through a crazy series of transformations: first the lean, mean XLR8, then the sparkling Diamondhead, followed by a drooling Wildmutt, and then Four Arms.

'Hey, what's going on?' Ben cried out.

'The power surge must have affected the watch!' Grandpa said. Ben was not complaining. As Four Arms, he finally had the power to wrench himself free from his bonds and trash Vilgax's nasty device. It was payback time.

The whole spaceship was now in a state of high alert. Just as Gwen emerged from The Rust Bucket, a swarm of flying drones zoomed into the control room, blasting everything in sight. They were determined to zap the intruders even if they had to wreck their own ship to do it.

'Look out!' shouted Gwen. Four Arms didn't need to be told – he had the power to reach out and swat these little pests like mosquitoes. He raised a mighty pair of fists; he was going to enjoy this!

BLEEP! The Omnitrix flashed and Four Arms morphed into the phantom form of Ghostfreak. Now his grey, ectoplasmic fists flew straight through the drones, with all the impact of a light summer breeze.

'Oh, man!' groaned Ghostfreak in his creepy voice. The drones slipped through his spooky body and continued their rampage. Another explosion shook the ship – the power surge was causing a system overload on a massive scale. Vilgax's battleship had never faced such a crisis before.

Before Ben could figure out his tactics as Ghostfreak, the alien ghoul morphed into the tiny, bug-eyed form of Grey Matter. The drones circled round for another wave of attack.

Grey Matter leaped on-board a passing drone, creeping into its workings. He used his incredible alien brain to make a few smart changes to the programming. **KA-BOOM!** As Grey Matter jumped to safety, the device self-destructed, showering metal fragments on all sides.

'A little alien know-how, and the toaster is toast,' Grey Matter smiled to himself. But the mini genius didn't hang around for long. **BLEEP!** Now Ben had morphed into Upgrade. Gwen, caught in the middle of all the action, was trying to take cover – but she was directly in the drones' line of fire. Ben had to do something quickly, or his cousin could soon be history!

Like a big black jellyfish, Upgrade slurped into the workings of the next drone that passed by. This one was the daddy of them all. Upgrade invaded the drone's systems, changed its core program and morphed it into a gigantic floating buzzsaw. It spun round crazily, cutting up every other drone that came its way.

'Try picking on someone your own size!' Upgrade said. Grandpa Max was getting in on the action too, using his giant laser cannon to take out more of the robots. Against all the odds, it actually looked as if the Tennysons were winning this battle.

KA-BOOM! A power surge blew another hole in the side of the hull. The room tilted. The spaceship gave a sickening lurch, then went into a nosedive – down towards the Earth. Grandpa Max's face told Gwen how dire their peril had become.

'I've got to get the ship under control!' Grandpa Max said. He raced over to the nearest monitor station, studying the screens and read-outs like an experienced astronaut.

Nobody had noticed a huge, dark shape rising up out of the smoke in the smashed-up control room.

'He can fly a spaceship?' asked Upgrade, looking at Grandpa Max with bewilderment. Gwen grinned, while taking a drill to a passing robot drone.

'At this point, nothing surprises me!' she replied.

WHAM! Vilgax was back. He smashed Grandpa Max clean across the room, almost through the gaping hole The Rust Bucket had made in the other side.

'Grandpa!' Ben and Gwen cried in one voice. Vilgax stomped Grandpa Max to the ground, holding him down under his armoured boot. Grandpa groped for his fallen laser cannon, but it was out of reach.

'Your weapon won't help, Tennyson.' Vilgax sneered. 'As you can see, I'm much stronger than I was at our last encounter.' The towering alien raised a cruel claw, ready to strike a final blow.

'Nooo!' Upgrade hurled himself at Vilgax,

hit him at full speed and sent them both tumbling out of the hole in the wall.

'Ben!' Grandpa Max cried.

The stone face of President Abe Lincoln looked on as Vilgax plummeted past him and smashed into the ground. Upgrade was far luckier. He morphed his body until it was as thin as a parachute and was now floating happily on the breeze.

BLEEP! Upgrade suddenly morphed into Ripjaw – a big, heavy amphibian. Ripjaw could definitely not float on a breeze. He crash-landed on President Lincoln's nose with a painful thud.

'Sometimes I hate this watch,' snarled Ripjaw. Using all his strength, the razor-toothed alien hauled his pale-white, scaly body all the way up to the top of the head. There he lay, gasping. Ripjaw had one, fatal weakness.

'Can't breathe,' he panted. 'Need water!' A dark shadow fell over Ripjaw's helpless form.

'You are a slippery little fish, child. But no longer.' Vilgax stretched out a claw towards the Omnitrix – but there was a sudden whoosh. Ripjaw had vanished.

Vilgax spun round, confused. There, zooming across the presidential heads behind him, was XLR8, his sleek body, stripy tail and black pointy head glinting in the sunshine.

'I can still give you a run for your money!' quipped the speedster. But Vilgax didn't believe anything could get away from him. Bounding with unbelievable speed, he launched himself after Ben.

The alien came to a halt on the head of President Jefferson. He looked from side to side. Impossible – his foe had completely disappeared!

'You can't hide from me forever, boy!' Vilgax roared.

'Wasn't planning on it! Peek-a-boo!' XLR8 called out. There was a cloud of dust, a roar like a tornado, and XLR8 raced towards his enemy at ramming speed. He hit Vilgax with maximum force, bouncing back on impact. Vilgax hardly even registered the attack.

'Urgh,' groaned XLR8. 'I'm gonna feel that tomorrow.'

'For you, there is no tomorrow,' growled Vilgax, bringing down his mighty fist. XLR8

streaked away in the nick of time, and the alien was pounding dirt again.

'You can't escape me,' Vilgax said, bearing down on his foe, fists flying. Finally, he caught hold of XLR8, swinging him round and hurling him into the rock face. Clouds of dust filled the air but, when they cleared, XLR8 had gone, and a being of glistening green crystal stood before Vilgax.

'Special delivery!' said Diamondhead. The green hero unleashed a two-fisted attack, battering Vilgax with his diamond-hard fists,

SMASH SMASH SMASH! The alien hardly flinched. Diamondhead looked down. That shattering sound had been his own fists. He was now battering Vilgax with two broken stumps.

'Oh, man! I guess I should've seen that coming,' said Diamondhead. He looked up and saw his enemy about to pummel him into the ground. This time there was no escape. As he braced himself for the blow, Diamondhead heard a faint **BLEEP**.

WHOOM! Vilgax's fist passed straight through Ghostfreak and hit nothing but the ground.

'Yesss!' whooped Ghostfreak, in his creepy voice. 'Sometimes I love this watch!' The one-eyed phantom sank into the rock and passed safely through the other side. At last, Ben had escaped his relentless attacker.

Grandpa Max and Gwen sat side by side in The Rust Bucket, ready for the drive of their lives. The great spaceship had finally hit the earth, ploughing a mighty furrow across the South Dakota plains. Robot drones squawked, panicked and collided on all sides.

'Better hang on to something,' Grandpa Max warned. 'This might get a little bumpy.' He grinned and put his foot down.

Gwen could hardly bear to look. Grandpa activated the battering ram and powered the six-wheeler through the walls of Vilgax's ship, smashing everything in its path. Gwen shut her eyes as they ripped through the hull again and flew towards the green grass of planet Earth.

There was a loud thump and a screech of brakes as The Rust Bucket hit the ground and screamed to a halt. They were out. Behind them, the vast spaceship lay jammed into the ground. Grandpa Max and Gwen sighed. They were both still in one piece, but shaken.

'You all right, Gwen?' Grandpa asked. His granddaughter nodded.

'At times like this, going back to school doesn't seem too bad,' she said. Then they heard heavy footfalls stomping towards the vehicle. Gwen looked round, hopeful.

'Ben?'

Ghostfreak slipped through the rocks as only he could. There was smoke and dust everywhere from the crash-landing of the spaceship. Suddenly, he spotted a familiar sight in a deep rut up ahead – The Rust Bucket.

'Grandpa? Gwen?' Ghostfreak phased through the back of the vehicle and searched it. There was no sign of his family. When he emerged through the front of the van, he immediately discovered what had happened to them. Vilgax was standing in front of him,

Grandpa Max in one claw and Gwen in the other.

Ghostfreak morphed into Wildmutt. The big orange alien-hound snarled furiously, its fangs dripping and its powerful hind legs crouched and ready to spring. But he didn't attack. He knew it was hopeless.

'It's your choice – you, or them,' Vilgax said grimly. Wildmutt seethed with anger, then backed away and hung his head. Vilgax tossed

Grandpa Max and Gwen aside, then touched Wildmutt's Omnitrix symbol. The ferocious creature instantly morphed into Ben.

'How noble,' said Vilgax, carrying the helpless figure of Ben towards his crashed ship. The big alien lumbered through a hole in the shattered hull of his vessel. He was astonished to hear a familiar voice shouting after him.

'Vilgax! No! Don't go back in there!' It was Grandpa Max.

'Foolish Earthling,' he sneered, dropping Ben to the floor. 'Why would I –' then his words dried up. He had seen the warning lights flashing inside his ship.

'The auto-destruct sequence has begun!' he hissed in disbelief. A giant metal piston was pounding away in the control room, pumping explosive materials into the ship's power core. The ship lurched into the air.

Vilgax raced to his control console. He tried to turn off the auto-destruct, but his only reward was a massive energy shock. Ben slipped into the shadows and sneaked towards the giant laser cannon that Max had dropped earlier.

'Tennyson! You are the thorn in my side!' Vilgax raved. **ZA-AP!** Suddenly, he was rocked by a colossal laser blast. He crashed to the floor, the massive piston collapsing on top of him. Ben stepped forward, barely able to carry the enormous smoking weapon.

'Guess it runs in the family,' grinned Ben. Vilgax, his strength sapped by the ray,

struggled under the fallen piston, unable to escape.

'Noooooo!' he roared. The warning lights were still flashing, and the damaged ship careered across the sky. It was now so high that the air pressure was already sucking broken drones through the hole in the hull. Ben morphed into Heatblast and leaped after them.

He made it just in time. **KA-BOOM!** The ship exploded, torn apart in a blinding triple fireball.

Heatblast surfed a streak of fire towards the ground, triumphant. He hit the ground like a comet, ploughing a great smoking trench in the beautiful South Dakota countryside.

Moments later, Gwen and Grandpa Max raced on to the scene, stumbling through the smoke and mud, desperately looking for Heatblast.

The fiery hero was there no more. Perched on a pile of mud, calm as you like, was a happy

ten-year-old boy – Ben. Grandpa Max and Gwen rushed towards him. Ben turned, his face aglow with the reflected heat of the great inferno in the sky.

'Not bad for a doofus,' smiled Gwen. Ben grinned back. Then he gave Grandpa Max a long, thoughtful look.

'Grandpa,' he said. 'We need to talk.' Grandpa Max gave a knowing smile. When it came to secrets, he hardly knew where to begin.

BOOK COLLECTION

HAVE YOU SEEN THEM ALL?

Title	ISBN	Price
Ben 10 colour storybook 1 (And Then There Were 10/The Krakken)	978 1 4052 4165 6	£3.99
Ben 10 colour storybook 2 (Permanent Retirement/Side Effects)	978 1 4052 4166 3	£3.99
Ben 10 Annual 2009	978 1 4052 3909 7	£6.99
Ben 10 Scratch and Show	978 1 4052 3887 8	£3.99

Ben 10 Sticker Action	978 1 4052 3881 6	£3.99
Ben 10 Alien Hero Handbook	978 1 4052 3886 1	£4.99
Ben 10 Touch Screen Activity Book	978 1 4052 4523 4	£4.99
Ben 10 chapter storybook 1 (And Then There Were 10/Kevin 11)	978 1 4052 4467 1	£3.99
Ben 10 chapter storybook 2 (The Alliance/Secrets)	978 1 4052 4468 8	£3.99

COMING SOON . . .

2 COOL BEN 10 COMIC STRIP BOOKS!

And Then There Were 10	978 1 4052 4663 7	£4.99
Washington BC	978 1 4052 4664 4	£4.99

AVAILABLE FROM ALL GOOD BOOKSHOPS OR ORDER DIRECT FROM WWW.EGMONT.CO.UK